SPYMASTER

CONNOR WHITELEY

No part of this book may be reproduced in any form or by any electronic or mechanical means. Including information storage, and retrieval systems, without written permission from the author except for the use of brief quotations in a book review.

This book is NOT legal, professional, medical, financial or any type of official advice.

Any questions about the book, rights licensing, or to contact the author, please email connorwhiteley@connorwhiteley.net

Copyright © 2024 CONNOR WHITELEY

All rights reserved.

SPYMASTER: A WOMAN OF WAR

BY DOCTOR ELIZABETH ROMAN-NORMAN

AUTHOR'S NOTE

Dear Lord Inquisitor,

I am most honoured that you considered and rather harshly demanded that I write this book in some kind of effort to help flesh out your growing knowledge, the Inquisition's library and help answer your most burning questions about the current Imperial Spymaster.

As you know my Lord this is an area of immense research, passion and focus for me since the Imperial Spymaster, Catherine Roman, is my mother and it is only through research that I get to know her. Or maybe I am presuming your knowledge, if so I must apologise my Lord.

In case you are not aware, I haven't seen my mother since I was ten years old when she left me and my sister in the loving hands of two strangers (fellow agents) because she felt the only way to keep me and my sister truly safe was to defeat the traitors during the 9-month Crux War and help to make the Empire a safer place.

Of course my mother never returned to pick up her two children. I accepted that a long time ago because she wanted to protect the Empire and me and my sister even more by serving the Emperor. Of course, I was a very angry teenager and violent young man but then I found history and I understood one single thing that had always driven my mother in her actions.

Love.

It was her love that caused all of this and it is that love that I will never ever forget.

Therefore, as you wished my Lord, I have written this book including decades of research, interviews and inferring from the spotty historical records what actually happened during the Crux War.

Of course, it would be so much easy to simpler write some fiction and create vague historical accounts of what happened, but my mother would never love me if I did that, my own university education forbids me from doing it and I am fairly sure that you my Lord would send an assassin to kill me if I did so.

So I did not.

But by Throne it would have been a damn slight easier.

Therefore, my Lord I hope you find this book useful because this is the most accurate, complete and well-researched book on the Crux War in the Great Human Empire. Enjoy.

Forever your faithful servant,

Doctor Elizabeth Roman-Norman.

CHAPTER 1

Normally when it comes to exploring historical events, historians are always taught to start at the beginning but there are so many conspiracy theories, pieces of misinformation and lies surrounding the Crux war that it was next to impossible to find a beginning but I have found it. And that is where the Crux War starts and a young woman's life is changed forever.

Now a lot of people and scholars believed that Catherine Roman was a noblewoman, the daughter of someone rich and powerful or she had a boyfriend in the Empire Secret Service.

Looking back at these lies I have to admit that I can understand where they're coming from. They are all reasonable to presume and they are all utterly wrong.

Catherine Roman grew up in the Crux system and she always lived on Crux Prima, she was the daughter of a con-woman and her father died when she was two years old. So she didn't exactly have a lot growing up and she actually lived in one of the Prima's many slums.

A lot of people are shocked at this but it's true and she went to school as much as she could, focusing on science, maths and Empire Tongue of course she wasn't very good at any of these, except psychology and chemistry.

A lot of experts over the years have tried to explain why Catherine was good at these particular subjects and not others. Some proposed a form of dyslexia, others proposed she was just dumb (a complete and utter lie) and others simply didn't dare to comment on a sitting member of the Emperor's Council on Earth.

I believe the latter are the smartest people.

Everything started to change in Catherine's late twenties when she was a guest at the home of a diplomat. The female diplomat had been sent from Earth for an unknown purpose but given how the talk of succession and political infighting dominated the news of the Crux system at the time, it is reasonable to assume that the Diplomat wanted to tell the dying Planetary Governor to make sure her Will was fixed before she died.

Of course that never happened because the planetary governor had died six hours ago.

Catherine always described the party and being there as a guest as one of the most defining moments of her life because she hated it with a passion. She had always loved the stunning bright golden walls, smooth art on the walls showing the best features of the galaxy and the brown wooden chairs were wonderful when compared to her own flat.

The people at the party were very kind, posh and snobbish. Catherine made notes in her diary later that night about how awful the women looked in their black silk dresses by describing them as black eagles that looked like they wanted to strike down their pray but they were too constricted to do anything except painfully walk around.

Thankfully as a single woman Catherine didn't need to wear such a costume.

Equally she did mention how hot the men looked in their crisp white Empire Army uniforms. Because that was the real reason for the party.

In amongst the fresh smells of rosemary, thyme and juicy roasted slices of pork, Catherine joined in many conversations about who was going to be the next ruler of the entire system. The Crux system was always weird because the planetary governor of Crux Prima ruled all eight worlds instead of only the one.

Catherine met and chatted and even kissed most of the men through the night, but she wasn't stupid.

She was the personal guest of a Lord Admiral Collins who was technically in line but had withdrawn because he knew what was coming. He believed a war was about to happen in the Crux system.

Catherine had laughed at him multiple times

throughout the evening whenever he suggested it because she couldn't imagine someone actually having the balls to attack the Empire. But as the night went on and she heard groups of loyal soldiers and commanders plotting away, she believed it.

Catherine later wrote in her memoirs that she had never been more scared for her children than what she heard that night. The historical records, Catherine's own diary and even the later traitors convicted of their crimes never revealed exactly what was said that night.

However, if we take a step back for a moment and focus on the context, then there are a few simple guesses since similar conversations in other threats of war have been recovered.

The most likely conversation overheard was how the loyal commanders, generals and soldiers were going to install the Lord Commander of the Crux system as the leader. And if anyone opposed the Lord Commander then they would die.

And given how violent the Lord Commander was, I can just about imagine how scary that realisation would have been.

The second most likely is she overheard members of the planetary Senate creating some kind of plot of their own. This most probably wasn't to establish a democracy or to create an autocracy but anything is possible.

And the final option is that Catherine overall heard someone wanting to contact the traitors to see if they would help.

Of course, contacting the Superhuman Traitors of the Angels of Death and Hope would be a very extreme measure. Those foul beasts want to enslave humanity, kill the Emperor and annihilate the Empire.

That's why this would have been so terrifying to Catherine and it was even more scary when we consider that these *loyal* Empire Army people were willing to say such a thing in this company.

Normally a soldier would be tortured for saying such a thing but this person felt safe enough at the party to say it.

That should have spoken volumes about what was going on behind closed doors in the political war rooms of Crux.

So Catherine did the only thing she knew, she went to her best friend Lord Admiral Collins informed him of the situation and they started talking about resistance, spy networks and making sure that Crux remained in Empire hands.

Catherine was outraged at first that he was suggesting they needed to spy on their closest friends, allies and peers but she was eventually persuaded.

Originally they were going to meet the next day in his office to plot this out fully but then Arbiters stormed into the party and arrested Collins, all the Senators of the planet and even some of the Empire soldiers.

All of their bodies were found the next morning

with letters carved into their chests and they were arranged in a certain pattern that told Catherine exactly what she needed to do.

This World Ain't Empire No More. Let The Loyalists Burn.

CHAPTER 2

Whilst it would take a whole year after the Crux War for this information to come to light, I want to add in here to out of sheer interested of making sure you follow, my Lord, the war as it happened.

So Arbiter's Lodge was a massive log cabin based on the schematics from Old Earth. The photos of the Lodge were stunning with its large brown wooden logs rammed on top of each other, holo-art hung on the walls by the hundred and coffee tables and small seating areas were littered elegantly around the lodge.

A lot of grand meetings had happened in this lodge over the centuries but right now, we're only interested in a single meeting that happened seven days after the execution of Lord Admiral Collins and the senators and other loyal soldiers.

There were only ever two people in the meeting regardless of what the other records say (mainly because they were simply made up) and it was between Arbiter General Ash and Supreme Arbiter

Ahsley.

They were two brothers and this was a fascinating difference because this ultimately shaped the final outcome of the war in the bitter end, and 9 months later.

Ash was a very tall man that had been born in the rich towers of the planet's government, given a very rich education and taught the ways of the law, murder and espionage at a very early age. Yet what was amazing about him was that he tried to spend as much time *out* of the towers as possible.

He used to tell others before and during the war about how much he loved running through the muddy covered streets of Crux Prima, talking and mixing with the plebs of the world.

All because he wanted to understand the people he would be arresting in the future. No one understood it at the time that I fully believe that was the critical difference between the two brothers.

On the other hand, Ashley was always cold, brutal and snobbish. It was a very poorly kept secret that he hated anyone not born of noble blood, there were reports of him killing plebs from an early age but nothing happened to him.

And once he even hospitalised his brother as punishment for mixing with the carnal scraps of society.

The meeting we've interested in happened on a perfectly warm day, Ash had driven here himself to avoid detection so he was a little surprised to see so many tens upon tens of Arbiters in their black battle armour waiting outside.

And thankfully because Ash kept such good notes because he was an Arbiter first and foremost, and he wanted to keep a record in case a prosecution ever happened, I can share with you a lot of the conversation.

"What the hell is going on brother?" Ash asked. "The world is burning. The System is coming under attack from all different sides and I know you are behind it,"

Ash hated it when his brother offered him a seat on a long brown sofa in front of a roaring fire so he never excepted.

"The Lord Admiral, Senate and Planetary Governor are all dead," Ashley said. "I am Supreme Arbiter and this world now belongs to me. I will impose my Law as I see fit,"

"There is no law other than the Emperor's Law. What you are doing is treachery of the highest level,"

Ash later wrote about his brother extensively in court documents and there was a particular passage that I want to enter here since Ash's own words explain it a lot more than I ever could.

'My brother was not my brother anymore. The beautiful best friend of mine throughout childhood had died. When we were children we often played together, fought together and we really were the best of brothers. But what I saw in front of me wasn't a brother of mine, our parents might have supported his decisions if they weren't dead and buried thankfully, but I did

not. Arbiters protect the Empire, they do not destroy it.'

So as you can see there was a lot of hate and confusion from Ash about his brother but he didn't actually realise just the sheer extent of what was going on until now.

"The world is under my control like it or not. The Arbiters and the Empire Army have merged together and anyone who challenges me will be executed for treason,"

Ash laughed. "Brother, you cannot be that. The Emperor created the Empire Army to defend humanity from external threats. The Arbitration from internal threats. They cannot be the same,"

"It is a shame brother. It really is that you cannot be a part of my growing empire that will be free from the Emperor. I will give you one chance to leave now, there will be a blockade formed around the system in ten hours and the fighting and my control will stretch to all other planets in system. Leave now or if I catch you here again you will be killed,"

Ash never could believe what his brother was saying to him and Ash actually wanted to kill his brother there and then because he later admitted that it would have stopped the war immediately.

Ash never admitted why he never killed his brother at all during the war despite the six chances he got, but it's also worth mentioning that Ashley never tried to kill Ash even.

Other people tried very hard throughout the entire war to kill him but Ashley never tried. And I think the answer was simple, they were brothers and brothers don't kill brothers.

But when Ash left that day he retreated into the criminal underworld that he had hunted for the past two decades, his brother was now in control and the entire system was now under traitor hands.

And because Ash was a good Arbiter and he listened to illegal Inquisitorial channels he had learnt all about the traitor Superhumans so he figured they would arrive sooner or later and there had to be a resistance force in place before then.

So he set to work, creating a small network of friends and past foes who hated the traitors more than each other.

And that's when he discovered Catherine Roman. The woman that would change his life forever.

CHAPTER 3

Out of all of the interviews, research and statements I have read over the course of my investigation, there is one person that I confess is a complete and utter nob head.

You see Danny Balls was a very complex and hard-to-understand man. He was a former officer in Naval Intelligence who spent his entire life in the Crux system. It was his job to detect, execute and learn from threats in some vain effort to help keep the system safe.

That meant that Danny was a very clever, methodological and patient man, but no one actually liked him. He was fired from Naval Intelligence without a bullet to the head because he was a drunk, foul man that everyone just wanted to forget about, and he spent every single waking hour in the exact same chair at the exact same table in the exact same pub so he was a rather perfect target.

He was a perfect target for Catherine Roman.

You see the 9th Public House (a creative name I know) wasn't a very nice place at all and my visit to this establishment only proved my point. The thin wooden walls of the pub were so thin that little holes allowed people inside and out to spy on each other. The wood was riddled with disease, worms and that only spread to the bend metal tables.

The tables were plentiful and they were sort of arranged in neat rows but customers were always moving, shaping and banging into the tables to create a pub that suited their needs.

Yet Danny always sat on his particular table that was covered with stains of stale beer, dried blood and my personal favourite, dried teeth. No one ever knew why Danny kept ten dried teeth from ten different people on his table and because he died through the war we cannot ask him. But I suppose they could be from his fallen friends.

Yet that is purely a guest.

So exactly one week on from the execution of Lord Admiral Collins and the others, Danny was still drinking his way through his hundredth beer at two o'clock in the afternoon. The music was playing loudly and the whole place stunk of sex, stale beer and cheap spirits.

Little did Danny know was that over the course of the past week Catherine had been talking to her friends on the first two days. Formulating a plan and processing her grief over her dead friend and on the third day onwards she started to contact her friends and their friends about becoming her informants.

Now I have to admit that for a woman that wasn't well-known, wasn't in a position of power and wasn't well-liked by the snobbish military, nobility and more of Crux Prima. She was extremely successful and by the end of the sixth day she had spies in a stunning number of places.

She had spies in every single department of the Crux Government, most shopkeepers in the highest levels of the Capital City were informants and even two captains of the Empire Army were her informants.

That was a stunning achievement and it really just goes to show how talented Catherine was when it came to making people feel comfortable, trusting her and making sure she got what she wanted.

On the sixth evening, Catherine was reading me and my sister a bedtime story and there was a knock on the door, so she kissed us both on the head and put us to sleep. And then she encountered Ash.

For the rest of the night they spoke, conspired and agreed to work together to form the network that would save the Crux System from damnation, and extermination.

It wasn't until years later when my mother wrote her memoirs that it was revealed exactly how she felt about Ash. She admitted that he was stunning, sexy and very attractive and she wanted to use him in more ways than one.

And yet she focused the entire conversation

between them on the mission and how best to go about their spy network.

The only weird thing about this encounter is that it was the only time in my mother's memoirs that Ash was ever mentioned. Despite him being her right hand for the next nine months and how they reportedly fell in love and had a child.

That is something I will never understand about my mother.

So on the afternoon of the seventh day both Catherine and Ash went into the 9th Public House and found a very drunk Danny.

Catherine wasn't impressed at all with this so-called hero and the feeling was mutual. There was a lot of foul language exchanged between the two until Catherine offered to pay Danny's bar bill for the past week if he listened to her.

Ash hated this idea and fully believed she was crazy but Catherine never ever said something she didn't mean and she wasn't stupid. She knew that Danny's bar bill would bankrupt her completely and because of the new administration it would also get her arrested.

Yet Danny was fascinated by her confidence so he listened and the entire world changed for all three of them.

CHAPTER 4

When I started researching this topic and I focused on this meeting between Catherine, Ash and Danny, I was flat out amazed at how many thousands of books and resources and even holocasts were focused on this first meeting. There were thousands of errors in each of them but by analysing all of them I've managed to get a great understanding of what exactly was said.

This is critical to understand because Danny's involvement changed the fate of Catherine forever, Catherine had made an extremely expensive bargain and Ash was very uncertain about Catherine's suitability as leader if she was willing to do something as stupid as settling Danny's bar bill.

So as the three of them sat in the 9th Public House around a very small metal table covered in dried blood, teeth and other stains, Catherine just grinned.

"Your record was impressive to read," Catherine

said. "You've served all over the system, made friends everywhere and you know where all the old abandoned Empire systems are,"

Danny cackled at her.

Catherine later wrote at length about Danny's strange laughter because it never sounded normal. There were times when she believed it was always fake, or caused by a muscle damage but Catherine never cared in the end because what he would come to mean to her.

"My record is the same as thousands of others. You ain't very smart if you've come here," Danny said.

"Not so," Catherine said leaning back putting her feet up. "I know exactly what you want and I read about your last mission for Naval Intelligence,"

Danny stopped drinking the moment she mentioned that.

"See you can stop drinking when you want to. Operation Red Dagger, a simple op in theory. You arrive on Crux 6, assassinate a recently arrived traitor superhuman from the Hydra Legion and then disappear into the night,"

Even now me and Ash both were amazed at how Catherine just spoke about traitor superhumans like they were nothing, and traitor superhumans from the Hydra legion were masters in disinformation, lies and deceit. It was amazing she had the balls to speak of them so plainly.

"The Hydra Legion," Danny said taking another

massive mouthful, "foul liars. So yes of course I was set up. I went in with ten other men and we were going to be fine until the ambush,"

"And yet you completed the mission and then you escaped for twenty hours whilst superhumans hunted you down until help could arrive,"

"What of it?"

Catherine stood up and stretched for a moment. She didn't have a physical need for doing this so many doctors and her friends think she did this from time to time to make a dramatic effect or pause.

"You are damn good at what you do," Catherine said. "You took an Oath to serve the Emperor until death and I know what you want is to do that once more,"

Danny stared at his drink and then looked at Ash who was sitting next to him in silence.

"What do you say about this *woman*?"

Ash grinned. "I say she wants Crux to remain in Empire hands and she has the will to do it. The government, Arbiters and military are against the Empire now. It's up to us to stop them,"

"Ha!"

Catherine leant across the table. "Empire reinforcements will be coming as we speak. The Empire will not allow Crux to fall without a fight but they face a very deadly problem and I'm sure many Naval Intelligence Officers will die before Crux is returned,"

Danny spat at Catherine.

Catherine only laughed. "All Empire forces coming in and out of the Crux System will be annihilated if we don't run interference. We need to open as many battlefronts for the traitors to fight so it weakens them and their barricade around the system,"

"So," Ash said, "when the Empire does come the orbital fight and then ground preparation is a lot shorter,"

"And victory can be a lot less deadly for us and the Empire," Catherine said.

Danny always studied his drink before he finished it and Catherine knew from his body language that he was preparing to leave. And he never left his drinking spot before ten o'clock at night so Catherine had to keep him here.

She couldn't allow him to escape from himself, his past and his role in her spy network.

"What was your Oath to the Emperor?" Catherine asked.

"I will not say it,"

Catherine stood up and Ash sat even closer to him. They weren't allowing him to escape.

"Say it and you can go and I'll cover your bar bill for the past week,"

Danny didn't dare look at them. "I vow to always watch, listen and spy over the Emperor and his citizens until I die,"

As soon as the words left Danny's head he shook his head and smiled at Catherine then Ash.

Catherine stood back down and rested her feet

up on the table. "Now then I think we have a lot of planning to discuss,"

"Definitely," Danny said. "I'll tell you everything I know but we have another problem. Every abandoned base, gun turret and ammo cache I know about the Empire knows about. I'll be surprised if the Arbiters haven't captured all them yet,"

"But I don't want your knowledge about that. I want your skills as a spy and a people's person. When was the last time you contacted your old master?" Catherine asked.

Now one of the many problems with earlier books, holocasts and interviews on his meeting was that no one cared to explain what Masters are in Naval Intelligence, because they aren't what you think they are.

Instead Masters are retired Officers that were the best of the best. Normally they retire to pleasure worlds and fill their days with sex, games and other pleasurable activities but others don't do that.

Other Masters focus on teaching, exchanging knowledge and still focusing on the enemies of the Emperor. They no longer had access to the resources of Naval Intelligence but that never stopped them and Danny was once mentored by a Master before he traded in his life of spying for a pleasurable station on the moon of Crux 6.

"Not for years but I'll contact him. He gave me a secured number so I'll use that and see what contacts he can connect me with,"

Catherine loved that reaction because she finally had two amazing people on board.

Yet she never ever expected Danny to say what he did before she left without paying for the bar bill (because the bill magically disappeared since the bar owner overheard the entire conversation and wiped it clean).

"You have a son and daughter right?" Danny asked.

Catherine nodded.

"Get them off world now if you can or don't do this. If you want to rebel against the Arbiters, Army and Government, isolate yourself from your children,"

Catherine later wrote about wondering that each night of the past week and that was why she kissed and spend every spare moment with them. But just hearing such fear, concern and force behind Danny's words, that shocked her.

So as Danny called his old Master, Catherine knew she had to make a final choice.

She could either focus on the spy network and make the Crux system safer for her children at the cost of giving them up. Or she could live with them and live in a terribly oppressive world.

The choice wasn't as clear-cut as many people believed because she was a mother first and foremost.

CHAPTER 5

I actually remember what happened the next morning like it was yesterday because, well, a ten-year-old boy never quite forgets the day his mother leaves him and his sister forever.

I knew that my mother had been crying and having a very fierce conversation with Ash the entire night, she was constantly wanting to be a mother, wishing she didn't have to do this and she kept repeating how she wanted the system to be safe for me and my sister. At the time, I didn't know what was going on and it wasn't until I learnt the truth about her that I realised what she was going on about.

So like the good son I was I stayed put in my nice little warm bed with its bright blue sheets, staring at my little Emperor holo-action figure the entire night hoping that it would protect my mother.

We might have lived in the capital city and the sound of outside was always filled with gunfire, bombs and explosions ever since the executions had happened and the Arbiters had sieged power. But my mother was so good with technology that our flat managed to block it out completely.

My mother always worked hard to make sure me and my sister always felt safe, no matter how much of that safety was a lie and sheer delusion.

The next morning my mother came into our shared bedroom and my sister hadn't slept very well at all. She had wanted me to go out and ask mummy what was wrong but I didn't dare, and I knew that the Emperor would protect us in the end. And as a ten-year-old bought up on the stories of the Empire I truly did believe it.

And for the sake of not being executed for treason by the Inquisition, I will say that I still do now.

My mother looked like she hadn't slept for a single moment last night, she was still wearing her beautiful long blue dress, her golden earrings were perfect and her pearl necklace dazzled in the weak morning light.

She came over to me and my sister, put us on the same bed and read us a final bedtime story. That was when I knew that something was deadly wrong because mother never read a story to us in the morning, no matter how sick we were (we sang songs when we were sick) and it didn't matter how good we've been at school.

Stories were for bedtime.

We all laughed, hugged and enjoyed ourselves for the next half an hour, and I could have sworn that I heard Ash crying at the door but I was too focused on my mother to dare look at a stranger like Ash.

Then she kissed us on the head, told us that she loved us more than anything else in the entire universe and everything she did she did for us.

A man and a woman walked in smiling, they were young, smiley and they really did project an aura of kind trust at us. Mother started crying as she packed up our things and handed us over to the two people.

And as me and my sister left the apartment, I could only focus on my mother's cries and screams and regrets as she broke down at the heart-breaking decision to leave her children forever.

Just so she could keep us safe.

At the time I never realised what was happening, and I was happy for the next two days until the two retired Naval Intelligence Officers dropped us off outside a spaceport in the capital city and they were arrested by the Arbiters.

But they shouted at us to run. They put up a fight and I grabbed my sister and we ran.

We ran as fast as we could into the space port. We dived into the ventilation system and then boarded a random space station.

We were later found and given to an orphanage and I would never say we had a bad life. The orphanage was kind, helpful and gave us a good education but I was a bad kid.

My sister thrived, and she thrived so much she was recruited by the Empire Army as soon as she reached 18 to become a medic.

She was dead a year later after the superhuman traitors invaded her base and slaughtered everyone inside as a statement of hatred towards the Empire.

I was just an angry child and my final words to my sister were *I hate you. You're just like mother. Always leaving me behind.*

The words make me laugh now because they're stupid and my sister left me to protect humanity, the Emperor and the Empire which she did amazingly for those 12 months. And my mother, well, she's still protecting humanity even now with one of the most powerful positions on the Emperor's Council.

But that never happened to me growing up, I was in tons of fights, I hated the world and I hated my life. All I wanted to know was why my mother never came to collect me.

No one actually knows the answer to that question because all the interviews and historical documents show that what drove Catherine throughout the entire war was the simple fact that she could see her children again. But that topic never came up after the war.

Even in her own memoirs once the war finished she never mentioned seeing her children again. And it couldn't be because she didn't love them because if she didn't love us then it makes no sense why she continued protecting the Empire in even more extreme ways than before.

Something during the war had to have happened to my mother to make her decide we were safer away from her.

After my mother cried back in the flat for a whole hour, she forced herself to get herself together and she comforted Ash, because he later spoke extensively about how this moment in the war was the most upsetting.

This was a man that had arrested mass murderers, broke up families by an arrest and he would later see friends' bodies shattered. But the only thing he said that had bought him to tears was seeing a mother give up her own children.

That was what broke him.

But with Catherine's children safely away and Danny had contacted her informing her a lot of his old contacts were alive again and already infiltrating a lot of other planets in the Crux System, she finally had her spy network.

And the war was truly just beginning.

CHAPTER 6

Alexendar Conning had served in Naval Intelligence for two years before the war broke out, during that time he had become well known in intelligence circles as a zealot who loved the Emperor and loyalty more than his own wife. He had led entire intelligence campaigns and killed at least twenty traitor superhumans in his time but once the war broke out he turned traitor for two days.

Then he realised how awful Ashley was as the newly "appointed" Planetary Governor and he very quickly went back to serving the Emperor. So Danny contacted him and Alexendar rose up to become Catherine's Chief of Staff after two weeks on the job.

Whilst the first three weeks of the war was hellish on all sides because no one knew what they were doing, and Catherine was still learning how to run a spy network that didn't only span Crux Prima but the other nine planets as well. By the end of the first month of the war ended, the map, alliances and enemies were a lot clearer.

It turned out that only Crux 9 was a safe heaven for those loyal to the Emperor because the traitors had been wiped out of that planet very quickly.

That gave Catherine a lot of political power and she had gotten to know the Planetary Governor Caleb very well over the past three weeks, and he had agreed to supply her with weapons, food and whatever else her forces needed.

The problem though was the other planets in the system. All eight other planets were fortresses filled with traitors and Catherine's entire spy network on Crux 6 had been annihilated.

Now her diary entries about losing Crux 6 are actually rather light-hearted compared to later entries, and I think this is because at this point of the war she was very new at this. Everyone was. So it's logical to presume that she wasn't very familiar with all of her people, what the job took and exactly the type of risks were involved in this setup.

And that theory is supported by Ash's own hesitations in his own diaries for the first three weeks of the war and a number of other members of her inner circle. Alexendar included.

Yet at the end of the first month, Alexendar met Catherine in a very small metal bunker that their spy network was operating out of for the most part.

Alexendar had always hated the bunker because it was so small and depressing with its black metal walls, no artwork and no sense of joy. He did enjoy the metal holographic table that was from the earliest days of the Crux System being founded but besides from that he didn't like it here.

The air was reportedly very damp, there were always hints of gas, petrol and burnt ozone in the air. Something he was very glad to discover wasn't harmful when he bought a doctor friend of his into the spy network and his friend tested the air. Yet it still didn't help the taste of burnt rubber form on his tongue.

Thankfully the holographic table they were using at the time had a default recording function that was active, and whilst traitor forces never got a hold of it. I managed to recover it on my trip to the base, and I do second everything that Alexendar mentioned.

Alexendar waved at Catherine when she came him with Ash, both of them looked tired, a little annoyed and frustrated which was to be expected considering how badly Crux 6 was with mass murders and trials happening against former network members.

Each of them stood around the table and Alexendar bought up a blue hologram of Crux Prima with three particular zones highlighted.

"The red zone covering the south of the planet is controlled by the military. The blue zone in the east and north are covered by the Arbiters and the yellow zone is controlled by the Planetary Governor personally," Alexendar said.

Catherine shook her head. "And the central

regions of the planet are safe and free,"

"For now," Ash said.

Alexendar had hated how the central regions of the planet were heavily toxic to anyone and because of the war millions of innocent people had been forced into its deadly atmosphere.

"I have heard that the military is going to invade the central regions in the next day or two," Alexendar said. "Two spies working for the military confirmed this,"

Catherine paced around for a moment. "We need to use this to our advantage. Crux 6 is gone. The Military on this planet is only growing in strength so we need to decrease that strength,"

"I agree but how?" Ash asked. "We're spies. We aren't fighters and I told you our contacts in the local militias have gone silent,"

Alexendar always liked it how Catherine grinned when the odds were impossible and everyone else agreed she was crazy for wanting to try.

"We might not be fighters. We might not be heroes. We might not even be the winners in the end but the invasion of the central regions will cause millions to be imprisoned. Can we use that?"

"You don't want to save them do you?" Ash asked.

"Not directly. Can we identify the prison they'll be sent to and infect the systems with something?"

"Yes," Alexendar said. "I can infect the computer systems with a virus that would allow me to open prisoner doors at will,"

"That's how we can recruit and I'm sure the militias in the system would be grateful for the angry recruits,"

Whilst a lot of academics and survivors of the war had discussed, criticised and argued about the nature of Catherine's plan, I realise that most of the arguments and essays all miss a single critical factor. The people in the central regions were breathing in and being exposed to toxic air.

This air and environment would have killed them all within the space of two weeks and these people weren't moving. Survivors of the war confessed this.

They were happy to die of poison compared to fighting the traitors.

And Catherine and her network didn't have the resources to save them so they allowed the enemy to do it.

Of course the next day millions were captured, over ten thousand people died in the attack, another twenty thousand died in transportation to the prison but three weeks later there was a mysterious prison riot and millions of them were freed.

Over two million of these people ran into the makeshift warbands that fought the traitors and this mass recruitment is referred to in historical records as "The Emperor's Gift".

The warbands were armed, Catherine had a lot of friends now in the warbands and the military looked extremely weak in the eyes of the new planetary governor.

Little did anyone realise at this point was that the Lord of War, the leader of the superhuman traitors, heard of this event and he immediately started plotting a course to the Crux System.

Along with over ten thousand superhuman Angels of Death and Hope.

CHAPTER 7

Over the course of the next month, Catherine did extremely well for herself with the help of Ash and Alexander. She had still managed to hold firm her network in all the major military, government and Arbiter departments on each of the planets and this allowed her a massive advantage over the enemy.

Her spy network was responsible for allowing the warbands to assassinate ten high-profile targets, the leader of the traitor Empire Army and even Ashley had lost both his arms because of the attacks.

Similar results were found on all other planets that she had control over her network, and she was slowly starting to rebuild her network on Crux 6 but she admitted in tons of places that this was impossibly slow and this kept her up at night.

And even better Catherine had confirmed reports of Empire forces were starting to amass on Crux 9 in an effort to break the traitor barricade around the system.

Just things couldn't last forever.

Catherine was sleeping one day in her little private chamber that was nothing more than a small grey metal small box that used to be a storage room for weapons. There wasn't a clock, window or any piece of technology because Catherine didn't want it to be hacked and spied on herself.

She was sleeping very peaceful that night and a lot of survivors of the network from this time reported how great it was to actually hear her snore at night.

Until this morning Ash knocked at her door and he didn't even wait for her to say come in, she slept naked tonight but Ash really didn't care about that (probably the only time he didn't in the course of the war) because he grabbed her, threw her battle armour at her and basically dragged her to see Alexander.

Of course he was dead.

In the course of the night one of the spies in her network had killed him, her chief of staff and because Danny wasn't at the base, he was still on Crux 6. She didn't know what to do.

Now Ash mentions a lot in his diaries how stressed out he was because this was his worse nightmare imaginable. There were over one hundred spies in the base all working and contacting different spies inside enemy territory and now one of those friends was a traitor.

Amazingly enough Catherine was never concerned or allowed her emotions to cloud her judgement on this matter. Because this was the day she had been treading and she was terrified of this happening.

Because one of the main problems with Catherine's network is that recruitment was done by word of mouth. If a spy knew a friend that they thought would be good, they didn't need to contact Catherine and get her thoughts, they simply recruited them.

This is how the intelligence network fell apart on Crux 6.

And all throughout the war different sectors of the network were annihilated, rebuilt and annihilated again because of this very problem.

Catherine had tried many times to fix this but she always admitted that at the end of the day, they were only amateur spies. None of them were Naval Intelligence, Inquisition or even Arbiters to be honest. They were amateurs trying to do the best they could with the limited supplies they could.

And it was even worse that Catherine was struggling to fund the network now. She could barely pay her network let alone her inner circle and cracks on other planets were starting to show. Crux 9 tried to fund her as best they could but they never had enough money because of their own problems and in the end they were having to deal with more and more traitor cults springing up.

So by the time the murdered happened Crux 9 was no longer funding Catherine's network.

So because of the dire situation, Catherine focused on keeping the network safe, there were tons of new spies meant to be coming in today, there were new reports being sent in and there was even a high-profile and powerful Lord coming to meet her.

Catherine immediately sent out a signal invisible to spies inside the base, but clear to everyone else not to come in today and to go dark for 48 hours.

This decision ultimately saved the network because of what was about to happen.

Red flashing warning lights exploded and Catherine knew that she had seconds before she was swarmed, and because of the base's ventilation system she was sure the traitors were going to flood in knockout gas to kill them all.

So Catherine and Ash worked together to do three simple things. They backed up all their data and transferred it to a holo-stick that they each placed in a very uncomfortable area of their bodies, they erased the information including the names and positions of their spies from the base's computers and they ordered an evacuation.

The problem was the evacuation order deleted itself because of what the traitor had done to the computer systems.

Catherine and Ash both rushed to grab a gasmask from their supplies but it was too late.

Immense columns of bright white glowing gas poured down from the ceiling, veiling and smouldering and choking all of them before any of the spies could react.

Catherine tried to fight it but she couldn't.

And her world went black as she felt two hands grab her and drag her unconscious body away.

CHAPTER 8

Out of all of the historical records, interviews and books written by people who don't know what they're talking about, the next two days are a complete and utter mystery. None of the traitors, survivors or Catherine herself actually spoke about what happened.

However, because of the surviving records from other captured spies throughout the war I'm able to give you an approximate account of what could have happened. Yet it was strange how Catherine and Ash survived at all, and it's even stranger that whatever happened led them to be so shaken by the experience that they never spoke about it.

Even to each other.

By all accounts after Catherine recovered from the gas she would have woken up in an interrogation room controlled by the military. It would be a horrible grey metal cube with only a grey metal desk, two silver chairs and a holo-recorder inside it.

The room would have been soundproofed and many captured spies and loyalists throughout the room reported how much they hated the silence. And the military was very well-known for using the silence as a weapon against their prisoner.

Maybe the most damaging part of the experience when a person first awakens is the sheer smell of lemons, bleach and blood that fills the senses. It immediately disorientates them and it teaches the prisoner that people die very easily in these interrogation rooms.

Normally this leads to people caving in very short order and throughout the first four months of the war when the military-controlled areas were separate from the other areas. Over three thousand spies in the entire system confessed their sins, crimes and they agreed to help with the traitors.

This is why after two days and Catherine managed to escape (more on than later) she returned to freedom and heard about how Crux 7, 8 and 5 were completely lost to her.

She wouldn't find out how this had happened until after the war but a group of twenty best friends and spies turned on Catherine in exchange for millions of credits and a guaranteed good life.

They were all executed after the war after suffering extreme torture by the Inquisition.

The twenty best friends ran an operation were they would try to broadcast a transmission and get the loyalists to contact them. Then the traitors traced the signal, stormed the loyalist location and killed them all.

There were no prisoners on these planets. Only burnt corpses paraded through the streets to remind loyalists that the traitors ruled the planet. And the Empire had abandoned them.

Anyway, when Catherine woke up, I highly doubted she was too affected by smell and other psychological techniques the military used to disarm its prey. I think she was just too good for that but she would have been quickly disarmed in ten seconds.

Ten seconds later a very tall, muscle and attractive man would have walked wearing a holo-cloak that would make him look identical to Ash. He would be carrying a gun and ID that made him look like he had always been working for the traitors.

Now this was Catherine's fear. She wrote a lot about this in her recovered diaries because she knew that Ash was the new Planetary Governor's brother and up until this point she was always scared about him being a traitor.

So why did she let him so close to her heart and operation?

No one knows for sure and because of Catherine's memoirs never talk about Ash, we will never know. But I believe it's because she knew deep down that he wasn't a traitor.

Then the conversation once the Ash-look-alike sat down would have gone something like this.

"Everything is gone Catherine. I have told them

everything. All your agents are captured, forces are making their way across each planet killing each communication station and soon all Resistance Leaders on those planets will be dead,"

Catherine sat back. "I know you aren't him. The voice is close but not good enough. Your face is handsome like his but not good enough. And I know the military is scared of being taken over by the Arbiters and the Planetary Governor,"

"You will still die because you're nothing but a weak-willed Empire scum,"

Catherine laughed. "How does it make you feel to know your own freedom is about to be taken away?"

Catherine wouldn't have mentioned how she knew this because her main focus was always about protecting her spies in all the government departments and other places they had infiltrated.

Yet she had known for weeks about the Arbiters and the Government combining their land and now they were both focusing on bringing the military into the fold.

Up until now the three fractions had been apart and operating in unity but the leaderships disagreed with each other. Something that was starting to cause a lot of friction and the Planetary Governor wasn't having it anymore.

"Ash is already dead you know," the look-alike said.

Catherine tried to move. "Impossible,"

"Tell me Catherine, where are your remaining spies? Tell me that and your spies will live,"

Catherine shook her head. "That play will not work. Any bargains we make here will be undone instantly when the Arbiters take over,"

Then she noticed a minor flash of fear dance across the look-alike's face and this is where we do actually have historical records about what happened next, because Catherine had been knocked out cold for two days.

"Damn you," the look-alike said as he deactivated his holo-cloak, freed her and gave Catherine the gun.

She didn't even hesitate when taking it.

"I don't know how long I can protect you and your friends. You are right the Arbiters will move on the military soon and the military doesn't have the numbers to protect itself. Many in the military want to serve Ashley directly,"

Catherine hated hearing that.

"Go out the door, turn left and go straight down the corridor. If you keep walking and acting strong no one will give you a second look trust me. I set your friends free ten minutes ago. I saved as many as I could but you have to go now,"

Catherine nodded and thanked him. She later told investigators how she didn't know exactly how she knew to trust him but she did.

And it saved her life because a day later the military base was swarmed by Arbiters and a lot of the military staff died.

The man who freed Catherine was called Joey Cade, he managed to escape too and he spent two months travelling around Crux Prima trying to free as many captured spies as possible.

He didn't survive the war. He was shot in the head two months later when he tried to save a group of young women from being firebombed.

The historian Allison Oaks later wrote the following about Joey and I completely agree:

He might have started off as a monster but he died a hero, a saviour and much of the population of Crux Prima own their lives in some small or large part to Joey. He died unremembered but his actions saved a lot of lives. Including Catherine's own.

A single action that saved the entire system.

CHAPTER 9

Catherine was freed at the end of the second month of the war and the third month didn't exactly get much better for her. Her network was mostly destroyed, she had lost all her spies in the Arbiters and she was bankrupt.

Catherine could no longer support her network financially so by the end of the third month the only planet she had an organised network on was Crux Prima. There were other spy networks on the other planets but they were nowhere near as effective, organised or impactful on the war than Catherine's.

There's been a lot of discussion about why this was and even by the third month, the reasons about why Catherine's network was so effective had become very clear.

It wasn't because of money, power or influence. It was because at the end of the day, Catherine was the head of her network and she had impressive skills when it came to convincing people to work for her, she knew how to handle impossible people and she truly believed in what she was doing.

She had such a fierce drive that she was impossible to stop and the third month seriously tested her.

Each week of the third month she would arrive at a new safehouse, set up base and try to rebuild her network. She updated protocols and taught her staff new tricks so they wouldn't get a traitor into their network again but it didn't work.

Each week she would be attacked, assaulted and worse.

At the very last safehouse she used at the end of the third month, she always confessed that this was her favourite because it was like the house she grew up in as a child. A lot of scholars falsely believe that she wasn't lying here and she was only pretending this wasn't her childhood home, but I spent a good few summers in that house and that burnt down when I was 8 years old.

The house was a very large wooden one with polished log walls, a blue carpeted floor and there was an immense fireplace that Catherine loved. And it also contained a hidden escape hatch that Catherine and others used to get in and out of the house repeatedly.

So she was working away in her office using her own private dataslate and reading a new battle report about the exact date and time about when the Arbiters and Government were finally going to invade the military-controlled areas.

It was a week from when she read about it.

And that posed the most important threat to her network and her safety because she had received a few reports about the military helping her agents over the past month. It seemed that they wanted to survive and go back to Empire rule but they couldn't say it publicly.

And it was even worse that the Empire fleet trying to break through the barricade around the system wasn't working. Progress was too slow so Catherine really wanted to infiltrate the traitor fleet and hope that would help her cause.

Gun fired ripped through the house.

Catherine leapt up. Ash dived inside. He locked the door.

The office didn't have access to the fireplace and escape hatches. They needed a new plan.

Arbiters were raiding the house. A lot of the network had escaped but twenty had already been captured and the Arbiters knew that Catherine and Ash were in.

They agreed to split up and some mentioned that Ash kissed Catherine here but that was never confirmed.

Arbiters smashed down the door. Catherine jumped at them and an Arbiter slapped her across the face.

Ash dived on them. Catherine escaped in the confusion and loyal spies to her found her a few hours later in a nearby town.

Over the forth month of the war, Catherine reported that there was a lot of problems for her during this time because something didn't feel right.

She had set up shop in a little flat in the capital city and now that she was a Most Wanted fugitive in the system, she could never leave the flat.

Thankfully the flat was very nice if not a little small. It had a wonderfully well-stocked kitchen, living room that Catherine spent the first day disabling all the technology in there and it had one bedroom. She never slept in it as she was concerned about enemy raids at night.

And she believed she could better defend herself in the living room next to the front door than in her bedroom.

She was proved right once about that argument at the end of the fourth month.

Using the flat as a base she managed to get agents and spies into the traitor fleet of ships that were attacking and managing to keep the Empire forces at bay.

The highest-ranking spy she managed was a Captain General Hunter O'Beck and he was in charge of ten destroyers.

Originally the plan had been for Hunter to cause a fight to breakout during a battle where his destroyers would attack the traitor forces.

This never happened because as Catherine found out in holo-news two hours later, Hunter was captured, his spy friends were captured and they were fired out an airlock.

Catherine had lost all the spies she had in the navy fleet in a space of two hours and it was even worse when the traitors realised how she had done it. And they killed two hundred other soldiers who *could* have been converted to loyalists.

Catherine never truly forgave herself for those two hundred deaths because she was happy about them in the sense they were two hundred less traitor soldiers to fight, but she was angry with herself because they were simply soldiers. They weren't evil, corrupt or anything.

She also lost the full support of the military and warbands by the end of the fourth month because the Government and Arbiters had finished consolidating their power. Now Crux Prima and the entire system only served Ashley and Ash was still nowhere to be found.

It turned out during this period he was running extremely high-risk ops against his brother with a lot of success but Ash was captured towards the end of the fourth month.

He escaped two days later but this is widely known as the beginning of the end for him.

And even though Catherine had no idea if she was coming or going or if she had a leg to stand on by the end of the fourth month, she later wrote the following about a single event that truly scared her.

The Angels of Death and Hope arrived on the final day of the Fourth, their ships were so massive in their blade-like construction that they turned the entire planet black for a full five minutes.

I didn't know if the sun would ever return. I didn't know if the superhumans were really on there or what. Ashley didn't know either and the entire planet was shocked to the core as thousands of blade-like drop pods descended by murderous screaming Angels towards the ground.

The Angels of Death had arrived.

CHAPTER 10

Interestingly enough the first half of the fifth month of the Crux War was called amongst the innocent citizens of the system as "The Heralding Of Darkness" and I couldn't think of a better name myself because it really does sum up just how bad the war had gotten now.

Ashley had gotten extremely paranoid since the arrival of the Angels and whilst the Lord of War himself wasn't amongst them. These Angels were still his legion so all of the thousands of superhumans in the system were cold, cunning and extremely dangerous.

Some diaries and holo-vids were recovered a few weeks after the war and there was a particular vid that demonstrated just scared Ashley actually was.

And before I share with you the details of that vid, let me just remind you. At this point in the war, the death toll across the nine planets were nine billion, everyone who wasn't loyal to Ashley was on the run or dead, and Ashley himself had just ordered the complete bombardment of a refugee centre.

Two thousand burnt alive.

Ashley wasn't a man above committing mass murder for the sake of power, and whilst the real numbers are very cloaked and we will never know, it is wildly believed Ashley murdered twenty of his top commanders himself.

Most of these commanders and generals and captains were murdered simply because they were popular. Popularity was a dangerous threat to Ashley so he always sought to kill it in the most graphic way possible.

Even now in the modern era, Ashley is still referred to as the Blood King or Ashley The Red, because he killed so many people for no reason. And it was later discovered that Ashley had an entire maze built under his capital building for the sole purpose of unleashing hostages, spies and loyalists so he could personally hunt them down and slaughter them.

With there even being some evidence of cannibalisation.

Later holo-vids revealed (and psychologists are in complete agreement here) that Ashley had got completely insane and he would have gassed the entire system if he had remained in power. And if Catherine hadn't of stopped him.

Yet there was one holo-vid where Ashley remained sane enough to govern in the extreme, and it was a recorded meeting between the Planetary

Governor and a military general that he had murdered four days after this recording.

General Willow Winston was a strange character throughout the entire war because her loyalties changed once monthly. First she was loyal to the Emperor, then the Arbiters, then the military and finally the Arbiters and then personally the Planetary Governor.

She never seemed to care about the war effort, Crux Prima or anything besides from her own self-interest. Even the people who served under her and alongside her never understood what actually drove her.

Yet somehow she managed to run the military for a space of three weeks (making her the longest-serving Military General of the war) and she met Ashley in his office one afternoon.

I'll admit the office itself was strange judging by the holo-vid but it could easily be described as a large oval chamber with a high domed ceiling made from polished oak filled with weapon racks, a golden desk and a chair made from skulls.

This is the moment when psychologists believe he started to descend into madness. And soldiers actually stopped going to see him for the sheer hell of it, they only went to see him if summoned.

No one wanted to be summoned. Especially when rumours flew around of Ashley eating the soldiers if he got hungry. These rumours have never been confirmed but I personally believe them because if you watch the holo-vid closely the desk chair gets bigger and bigger with more and more skulls and bones being added overtime.

"You wanted to see me my Lord," Willow said, wearing her standard black military uniform.

Ashley just stared at her and he was wearing a very fine thick black silk robe he harvested off the body of the last planetary governor.

"Where are the Angels?" Ashley asked looking around like they were in the room with him.

"They returned to their ships this morning. They captured two hundred citizens for *testing* my Lord. I believe they want to convert them into superhumans,"

"Damn Angels. They scare me. Scare me I tell you. They want to rule Crux for themselves and their damn mindcamps,"

Willow shivered at the mention of the mindcamps. Immense structures and sometimes entire planets dedicated to the brainwashing of loyal servants so they became mindless drones for the Lord of War's will.

"We have sworn an oath to serve the Lord of War," Willow said. "We must serve the Angels and you once said you would never serve the enemy,"

Ashley laughed. "You think we would withstand the might of the Empire and the Traitor Angels. You are a fool but my days are numbered. We have to make a plan,"

"We are out of options my Lord. You allowed

the Angels free reign. *Our worlds are your worlds and everything of our is yours.* They were *your* words *Planetary Governor,"*

"Damn you! Damn you Willow,"

After that the holo-vid cuts out and I suppose it's only natural that she was killed four days later but it really goes to show how fragile the situation was on the planet and in the system.

It's impressive from a historical perspective to see how such a mighty dictator could actually fall into a scare little mouse. Because it's very clear here that there was a real turning point in the war.

And Ashley was no longer on top and this is later confirmed by a Supreme General of the Traitor Forces called Lord General Omar taking over the system in the name of the Lord of War.

Now this is even more dangerous when I checked with survivors of the war and found that they had a name for the new ruler.

They called him the *Killer In The Darkness*.

CHAPTER 11

If the first half of the fifth month was called "The Heralding Of Darkness" then the second month and the sixth month had to be called "The Darkness" and everyone all over the system knew it.

Catherine absolutely hated how the Angels had cut off her network from each of the other planets and there were tons of new restrictions that made her mission next to impossible.

After almost getting caught five times over the past 90 days, Catherine managed to gather her remaining forces (a mere twenty-two spies) together in the abandoned stronghold of a research base. Catherine had always enjoyed exploring the old bases and research ones were her favourite because they were immense hexagonal metal structures that were bomb proof, had excellent radar abilities and they all had weapons.

After setting the base on full alert, which Catherine knew would have the enemy suspicious and she knew without a shadow of a doubt that traitor Angels would be coming for them, she gathered her forces in the docking area which had a massive calm but fast flowing river a few metres under it.

All they needed to do was jump in the river, try not to drown and hopefully escape.

The docking area was massive with dirty metal walls with dents in, flickering lights that Catherine had broken on purpose and a great view of the lights of the nearby city.

Catherine had thankfully found Ash with a now-healing broken arm earlier in the month and she now knew that she had to formulate a plan or she would die.

As brutal as the past month had been with the Angels extremely cracking down on her network and capturing entire sectors and regions of the network, she had managed to send large amounts of information to Empire forces who were attempting to break into the system.

The Empire forces were getting less and less by the day and the traitors only seemed to be growing in number. The Empire had managed to destroy ten high-priority targets because of Catherine's intel but it was still slow progress in orbit.

The only major progress the Empire had made was the recapturing of Crux 8 and 9. Those two planets were fully in Empire hands and all traitor forces had been defeated.

The following meeting transcript was derived

from what a number of survivors mentioned and Catherine's own memoirs reinforced what they said. So this information is highly accurate.

"We cannot be reactive anymore," Catherine said. "We need to fight back hard and faster. We need to re-establish the links with the other planets,"

There were tons of whispers and quiet words amongst the remaining spies.

"We have lost all our other spies in the government, departments and orbit. All murdered by the Angels. We need to be quick if this war is going to end with an Empire victory,"

Everyone frowned at Catherine.

Catherine loved each and every member of her network and as much as the network believed in *her*, they all later admitted that their belief in the cause was basically dead at this point.

They could barely eat, afford heating and live any sort of basic life. A lot had even considered joining Ashley just so they could get three meals a day.

It was that bad.

"We can do this," Ash said. "We can win this war. The Empire can rule over us again and the Crux System can be powerful,"

"But how?" one man asked.

"Because it is the Will of the Emperor," a woman said called Marie Aner and she was always described as an attractive woman with model qualities and an extremely fit body.

Catherine was stunned that someone else spoke

so she waved Marie up to stand next to her.

"The Emperor gave us the vision, tools and Will to make this happen. He allowed humanity to colonise the stars and make the stars *our* home," Marie said.

Catherine nodded. "Exactly and it is the Emperor and our belief in him that must remain strong,"

"Because without the Emperor, humanity is nothing," Ash said. "And if we fail here then the traitors are one step closer to killing him and enslaving humanity,"

All three of the now-leaders paused for dramatic effect.

Then Catherine stepped forward and everyone stood up and smiled at her.

"We cannot allow that can we? For the sake of our children, our future and *our* Empire, we cannot allow the traitors to take it from us,"

Everyone nodded fiercely.

"Then," Catherine said, "we need to move quickly and dangerously on the communication tower two kilometres here. Our intelligence shows this is how the Angels are blocking us from transmitting to other planets and Empire forces,"

"But we're twenty-two people," a woman said.

Catherine laughed. "Exactly. My plan is simple and it includes this river but it's dangerous,"

Catherine's plan was actually extremely intelligent considering how dire the situation was and she literally had one chance or she was done.

The entire network knew the Angels were racing towards them and unless they were acted quickly they were going to be captured.

So Catherine had rigged the research base to explode in such a way that the power supply that the base generated would be added to the river on a scale never seen before.

And bear in mind that the research base was calculated to have created enough power to light up all twenty-nine moons in the Crux System.

So add that to a river the size of a small village that was only connected to the Communication Tower two kilometres down river. That was going to have a hell of a firestorm.

But it was dangerous because Catherine predicted that large lighting bolts would shoot off the water because of a strange compound found in Crux water supplies.

She asked if anyone was against the plan as the thunder of Angel blade-like shuttles roared overhead.

Everyone shook their heads and Catherine ordered them to jump into the water and be out of it in two minutes.

They jumped.

Catherine and Ash stayed behind and three minutes later they jumped in the river and exploded the base.

They just about managed to climb out the water thirty seconds later the power supply fell into the river.

Catherine suffered a badly burnt hand but she escaped.

The entire network ran away as the deafening roar of an exploding tower screamed around them.

CHAPTER 12

Out of all the people to survive outside of Crux Prima, Danny was the only person who managed it and during the first seven months of the war he had travelled to every single planet except Prima twice or more.

He had met with Empire Commanders on Crux 9 after the liberation and as much as the Empire Commanders ordered him to remain on the planet, he didn't. He made sure he went back into the fight and it was on Crux 4 that he made his most important impact on the war.

He discovered something that Catherine would later recall as "the key to everything".

Now Crux 4 was a dwarf planet by Empire standards, it was made completely out of coal and the people living on the planet were extremely poor. Because coal had no purpose in the Empire, you cannot burn it, you cannot sell it and you cannot grow things on it.

Except Crux 4 was used as a research planet for centuries because it also had a lack of gravity that made it a place of fascination for physicists.

When the war broke out, Crux 4 was the first planet outside of Prima to recognize Ashley as the system's rightful ruler and Ashley visited the world (the only world he actually visited during the war) and Catherine's network never really gained a strong foothold here compared to other planets.

Yet Danny changed that by training up ten men and women to serve only Catherine and because of Catherine's messages of encouragement, guidance and training with these ten people. She turned them into an incredible small network.

Revealing the researchers on the planet were investigating anti-gravity weaponry.

Even all these decades later, the Empire still doesn't use anti-gravity weaponry and for those of you who do not know what this is, the only survivor of this cell described it as only working in two ways.

If there was gravity present then the weaponry would amplify the gravity by factors of millions and it would crush the object in seconds.

If there wasn't gravity present then the weaponry would add billions of tons of gravity, so yes before you ask I have no idea why all the files said they were researching anti-gravity.

It wasn't clearly a lie.

In the second week of the seventh month, Danny arrived on the planet to meet a leading researcher that was hoping to turn loyalist and he had vital information to share with Danny.

Danny was very cautious because he couldn't reach the ten men and women that he trusted on the planet.

When he arrived he was arrested by superhumans and taken to what the only survivor referred to as "The Death Room".

I visited the room in research of the book and it isn't as you would expect. It's still a very long room with a low ceiling and both the walls and ceiling are covered in a bright white plastic coating with slashes of bright red blood on the walls.

Yet besides of the blood on the walls it is a scarily calm and relaxing room. There's relaxing classical music playing in the background and the smell of roses fills the air.

Danny entered the room and now the historical records get very dodgy and there are a few pieces where I am sheerly guessing about what happens next. But that is rare.

The bodies of eight men and women were lying on the ground when Danny was strapped to the walls and icy cold metal chains were attached to Danny's wrists and ankles, and a post-mortem done on Danny revealed these restrains actually ate away at his joints.

Then a superhuman Angel wearing black battle armour styled on medieval knight armour from ancient Earth wanted to interrogate him.

No one can find out his name but he was

probably the nicest traitor Angel ever found but he was a sadist at heart.

"Where is Catherine Roman?" the Angel asked.

Danny never spoke. Never revealed anything. The Angel actually cut out his tongue in the end as punishment.

Whilst most prisoners on Crux 4 broke after ten hours of intense torture, punishment and beatings, Danny did not and even without his tongue traitor reports showed that Danny kept wishing Catherine was okay.

He allowed himself to go through so much torture to keep her safe.

Remember this is the exact same man that was a drunk, foul and argumentative man up until a few months ago. Never in Danny's life had he actually put someone else's life ahead of his own.

This is how powerful Catherine was in his mind.

When the traitor left after ten hours of torture, I know that Danny wanted to escape and protect Catherine. The traitors all knew that she was still on Prima and Danny had been working to get her off the planet.

All because he knew if she died the network died.

Danny struggled really hard to get out of the restrains that held him in place and using the post-mortem data I can tell you that Danny had very flexible wrists and hands.

So I believe he managed to make his hands very narrow so they could almost slip out of the restrains but they weren't narrow enough.

The post-mortem also shows his hands were broken or at least fractured. Doctors tell me the injuries on his body could have only happened if he had broken his own bones.

But Danny escaped and he really wanted to escape.

Then Danny would have had to go out onto a very long white corridor with bright white light that would have dazzled him, but Danny wasn't a fool.

He had been an intelligence officer for decades so he knew exactly how the Empire laid out its bases so he went to the control room.

Thankfully it was most certainly empty because there was no way I believe how he could have fought off Angels (superhumans) with broken hands.

Security data later revealed that Danny had spent about two minutes on the computer terminals in the control computer and he found evidence of the Anti-gravity project.

He sent the entire file to Catherine and survived the Angels long enough to make sure destroyed the terminal he was using to make sure her location was top-secret.

His post-mortem revealed immense trauma to his body that's why it took a year after the war to actually find out if this was Danny or not. His face was never rebuilt because most of the bones had turned to powder and the rest of his body wasn't in much better condition.

But the lesson remained.

Danny sacrificed, hurt himself and fought so hard to make sure he could send Catherine the information he knew existed on Crux 4.

Of course the ball was now firmly in Catherine's court.

And she was losing more and more allies by the month.

CHAPTER 13

Catherine absolutely received Danny's information at the worse possible moment because she and Ash were at a spaceport just outside the capital city and they had been stopped by a security guard. They were wearing holo-cloaks and they had covered their tracks the best they possibly could.

The guard had taken them into a security area which was a white wooden hall filled with scanners and there was a detainment box (another white metal box room) just to their left.

Catherine had wanted to react and knock out the guard immediately but Ash had told her not to and when I recovered security footage I got a lip reader to say Ash's exact words.

"We can't do anything not in your condition,"

Now believe me, myself and hundreds of other academics have studied this sentence and everyone agrees Catherine was not injured.

So she only could have been pregnant and whilst

she has never confirmed the birth, she also never denied it happened and she never denied the baby passed away.

I believe her and Ash had a child together and that was why she never mentions him again in her memoirs not since the day they first met. Because they clearly loved each other, they clearly had sex and they had a child together.

So why doesn't she mention the child ever in her books, interviews and in her real life?

Probably for the exact same reason why she never contacts me again or my sister before she died. Something in the war changed her mind about wanting her children back.

And that reason is something we will never know.

Anyway, in the security room the guard was inspecting Catherine's personal communication device when she got the information and at first the guard didn't care.

Then he must have realised what he was inspecting.

Catherine punched him.

Ash grabbed her and they ran stupidly into the containment room and they locked the door.

They were now trapped in a locked room, the guard was calling in Angels and the network was nowhere nearby.

Catherine didn't allow this to upset her or anything because she simply got to work and she didn't even deactivate the security camera in the room.

There was a chair so she sat down, placed her communication device on the table and she studied the hell out of what Danny had sent her.

Ash disabled the door's opening mechanisms but they both knew the Angels would be here to smash it down sooner or later.

"He's sent us plans for anti-gravity weapons. There's everything here including schematics for how to build them," Catherine said.

Ash smiled. "That's great. Can we build one to get us out of here?"

Catherine didn't answer for a few precious seconds but she was studying the data intensely like how a professional chef might study a fruit before deciding if it was truly as good as advertised.

She shook her head. "Negative but everything needed for these weapons is already board the Empire ships. It would take less than an hour to convert the cannons on them to anti-gravity ones,"

Ash was clearly shocked by the idea and Catherine knew in that moment that she had to get this information to Empire forces.

She might have been the head of the network and the Empire had sent her some schematics allowing her communication device to broadcast into space.

But she needed a clear signal. Being trapped in a containment room was not a clear signal.

Still she loaded up the schematics and pressed sent on the device just so the moment there was a clear signal the data would be sent.

Immense pounding dented the door.

Catherine and Ash shot up and looked around. There had to be another way out.

They both started banging on the walls and floor and ceiling.

Catherine's hands started bleeding she was banging so hard.

They both kept punching the walls more and more until Catherine discovered a hollow section.

She kicked it and a small computer reactivated for the first time in decades.

It updated for the longest minute of Catherine's life and then she hooked up her communication device to the terminal.

The door bent.

The shouting of superhumans filled the air.

The terminal connected to the spaceport's transmitter and she sent the information.

Seconds later the door exploded open.

Two superhumans stormed in.

Racing towards them.

There were no other guards.

Catherine and Ash flew backwards hoping to escape. They pressed their backs against the cold walls.

Ash jumped forward.

The Angels grabbed him and he shouted

something.

"Go!"

Catherine ran as fast as she could.

An Angel went after her but Ash kicked it in the head and then I will not repeat what I witnessed in the security footage.

I will just confirm that Ash was very dead, there was no body or bones left to perform a post-mortem or study later on after the war.

He was just dead.

The anti-gravity information had been sent, Catherine had escaped and the Empire had received the information and to say there were thrilled was an understatement.

The words of Lord Admiral Patch sums up the excitement perfectly:

Explosions were roaring around me as my first mate shook me so hard I thought the ship was about to explode.

She handed me the transmission from Catherine and it took me a minute to understand what it was.

I was so amazed at this incredible discovery that I ordered all forces to retreat immediately and we all set to work converting our cannons into anti-gravity cannons.

Then two hours later the war was changed forever. All because of one incredible woman that I had never ever met.

It was astounding, simply astounding.

CHAPTER 14

Whilst many Empire scholars stupidly call the moment when Catherine sent the data to the Empire fleet, the end of the war that doesn't reflect the reality in the slightest. It might have been the beginning of the end but by Throne was it the actual end of the war.

After Catherine escaped the spaceport, she ran through the tightly packed streets of the nearby city of Porta and she kept running. She kept bumping into people but because of the city's history as a space pirate stronghold up until five years ago she didn't meet any resistance.

In fact a woman grabbed her and pulled her into her pub where Catherine was given a hot meal (the first meal she had had in days) and was left to cry.

Catherine never wrote about this moment and in fact in her memoirs there's about a three-day gap between the death of Ash (again something she never writes about) and the next piece of evidence that she did something.

A lot of scholars don't choose to study this moment because as far as they're concerned the war is over.

However, I want to focus on this moment for a minute because whilst the female bar owner left Catherine in complete privacy because her bar was filled with patrons, I can only guess that she was upset.

Devastated even.

Catherine had been fighting, spying and resisting the enemy for months now. She never knew when or what her next meal was going to be in the past one or two months, her network was weakening by the day and the enemy had just gotten so close to her.

She might have not known but I suspect she knew deep down that Danny, a man and mentor that she wrote very fondly about and always spoke about him like a brother in interviews, he was dead.

And now Ash, the man she loved was dead, in the most horrific way imaginable and she was carrying his child.

I highly suspect that she broke here in the isolation of that bar and whilst when I visited the room where Catherine had been in at this time, it had been converted into a sauna. I could still feel the sadness in the room but that's probably just me projecting my wants into the room.

Yet we must remember that Catherine was a strong woman, probably the strongest woman the

Empire has ever seen and probably ever will. She was human at heart so she of course had moments of "weakness" but she was a servant of the Emperor so I doubted it took her long to recover.

Especially as I believe she still had that drive in that she wanted the war to end so her children could come back to her safely. This was even more important now that she was carrying her third and last child according to Empire records.

So she paid the bar owner, marched out of the bar and she rallied her network.

CHAPTER 15

Before the Crux War, Lord Admiral Patch was a literal nobody, there is barely any record of him before the war. I managed to find some evidence of him serving the Emperor on a lot of backwater worlds as a Captain and he ran his own ship a few times but he wasn't famous, well-known or even well-liked by the Navy.

When his ship was summoned into service for the Crux War, he was stunned, scared and he had no idea how to fight this war because his experience of combat was very limited. The only recorded encounter with the traitor forces I could find was a cargo ship attack that Lord Admiral Patch started.

He had never fought superhuman traitors, annihilator class warships and more. He hadn't even fought aliens before.

So I think the very fact that he was able to get into a position where he was the Lord Admiral of the Crux War just goes to show how stunningly desperate the situation was.

And how high the death toll was.

Another way to put it is the Empire sent a hundred thousand ships to the Crux system over the course of the war and in the end only 15% of the ships came back.

That was how bad the war was going for the Empire and Empire scholars believe without Catherine's aid that number would have been 0%.

So when Lord Admiral Patch received the information from Catherine and had modified their cannons to become anti-gravity cannons he ordered his forces to attack.

He didn't give a formation, he didn't give any orders and he didn't care what protests he got from his captains. He just ordered the fleet to zoom forward as fast as they could and fire as fast as they could.

It wasn't until two years after the war that Lord Admiral Patch was actually recognised as the military genius that he was. His strange tactic was good enough that it annihilated the traitor ships because they were surprised at the boldness of the attack.

And they were even more surprised and terrified at the new weapons that Lord Admiral Patch was using against them.

Patch didn't lose a single ship but he was still arrested by military police after the war for breaking rules, protocols and battle guidelines. Thankfully he was released two years later and he went on to have an extremely close relationship between his fleet and the Imperial Spymaster (also known as Catherine Roman).

The moment the Empire fleet shattered the barricade around the Crux System, Lord Admiral Patch ordered all the Empire Army and loyal Angel forces to prepare for a drop assault.

He knew there was no time to waste here so there was only ten minutes between him breaking the siege and the first drop assault involving two thousand Angels and ten thousand elite shock troopers from the Empire Army. It was a shocking first and brutal assault that led to the recapture of Crux 6.

Then under the command of Patch the Empire's forces basically became a rolling death ball sweeping over each of the remaining planets and slaughtering the traitors, and recapturing the planets.

Of course the hardest planet to retake was Crux Prima and Lord Admiral Patch admitted that this was the planet he was scared of, he had no idea how to take it and the enemy was so ingrained into the soil of the planet he knew this was going to be impossible.

Yet throughout the entire eighth month of the war, Catherine and her network had regrown and there were so many more members signing up all over the system because of the news of liberation was close.

Catherine was rather overwhelmed by the sheer amount of support she was getting throughout the system on all the planets, but her mission to her network was free.

We are no longer a spy network. We are a saboteur network.

Now that simple order has been debated in many academic papers ever since the end of the war because some academics believe this was a mistake and she should have left the action to the military but myself and others (including high-profile male Inquisitors) always believed these papers were sexist in nature.

And believe me, you do not want to read them if you're a feminist. Those papers are extreme at times.

Therefore, a lot of people believe this order is what actually ended the war because this is where we see communication, fuel and troop lines shattered in such a consistent way that on all the other planets except Prima that it was impossible for traitor forces to organise themselves.

And Catherine was extremely pleased when at the end of the eighth month traitor Angels retreated and fled the system, leaving Ashley alone, mad and we simply cannot understand his mindset at this time of the war.

His writing cannot be understood, his holo-vids were too crazy to look at and there is literally nothing reliable to understand him with. He was just crazy.

In the beginning of the ninth month, Lord Admiral Patch arrived in orbit of Crux Prima and the surprising thing was Catherine actually travelled up to meet him.

Lord Admiral Patch launched over twenty thousand loyal Angels and over a million Empire Army soldiers to the surface of Prima and the entire war was over in a month.

A very, very bloody month.

Throughout the ninth month Catherine admitted that she didn't find it an easy month because she was always expecting something to go wrong, she loved Patch's leadership style and both of them confessed how well they worked together and they were best friends by the end of the first week.

Whilst Lord Admiral Patch managed the ground assault, Catherine focused on analysing information from her network and this led to Patch's forces being very clever, cunning and always attacking the enemy from directions they least expected it.

The month was bloody but it was a great month in both of their opinions and Catherine really enjoyed working with Patch.

Ashley was found on the very last day of the month after loyal forces broke into his office. His body was smashed up over his desk.

A post-mortem revealed suicide was the most likely cause for his death.

The war was over.

CHAPTER 16

Because the war was really over after nine months, finding out what happened next was very difficult because resources, people and even security footage seemingly stopped recording the event of the war, but we do know a few things for sure besides from Patch being arrested and later freed.

Catherine was actually nominated as the new Planetary Governor of Crux Prima and at first she agreed to the position and she served as Governor for about a year. Amazingly enough what she did in one year was what it takes most Governors a century to complete.

She completely rebuilt the system from the ground up, she got hundreds of her trade deals and trade routes redone so over a thousand trading ships came through her system every week and her people loved her.

Even now there are statues of Catherine everywhere (and by Throne I mean everywhere), on the first day and last day of the way a grand celebration is held to honour Catherine's Day and even the Empire Army have a small minor celebration to honour her as well.

As well as the average income for a person in the Crux system went from 20,000 Empire credits to 100,000 after Catherine's first year as Governor but she resigned after the first year and she disappeared.

It was during the first year that most of her interviews were given, her memoirs were written and she was extremely popular back on Earth in the halls of Empire government because her deeds were so legendary.

But why isn't she well known in the Empire when other lesser heroes are?

I think there are three main factors. Firstly she wasn't born of noble blood and if we look at all the major Empire heroes that aren't from the Angel legions then it's easy to see they were nobles themselves. That was the first factor.

The second factor was that Catherine didn't care about being famous, whereas the more famous heroes went on a massive popularity campaign after their war efforts. They were on every single news channel, holo-paper and if there was a way to reach people they were on it.

Catherine didn't do that because she was focusing more on her people and the Empire.

Finally, Catherine wasn't liked in Naval Intelligence and the Empire Army and even Arbiters when she became planetary Governor. The people loved her but the officials who hadn't served her directly did not like her.

Many people from these hateful fractions have written a lot about their hate for Catherine and it all boils down to. She wasn't a noble, she never served and had Intelligence or any sort of Empire training and they were jealous.

So after she resigned and disappeared for two years, they did everything they could to discredit her.

It did and didn't work because she was still loved but she will never be remembered as the Empire hero she was.

So what happened to Catherine and her network?

All of the surviving members of the network were given a hell of a lot of power and responsibility until the day they died, they were generals, chiefs of government departments and all of them were very effective at their jobs. They were so gifted for the work that Crux is really incomparable to other planets because their productivity is so much higher.

Also Catherine fought day and night for months to make sure that the families of the dead members of her network got any kind of pension for their heartache. This is extremely expensive because so many people had died but after Catherine's other reforms and the increase in richness in the system no one cared about the price tag.

And this brings us to the present because Catherine has been serving as Imperial Spymaster on the Emperor's Council on Earth for decades now and the Empire stills stand strongly against the traitor, alien and mutant.

Of course we will never know exactly what's going on, I will never know what changed my mother's mind about coming to collect me and my sister but I do know that my mother loves me, the Empire and the amazing people of the Crux system.

She went through so much and fought so hard to make sure the system stayed out of traitor hands and for that I am so damn proud to be her son, and I really do love my mother for being Imperial Spymaster.

So now we all know what happened in the events of the Crux War, there were so many little events that impacted the war in minor ways but Catherine was the most important person and this book covered the most important events about her.

And Catherine is someone that the Empire should be very proud of and I'm really glad she's on our side, because if she wasn't then I hate to imagine the slim chances the Empire has at survival.

She's that good and I'm that proud of her.

GET YOUR FREE AND EXCLUSIVE SHORT STORY NOW! LEARN ABOUT NEMESIO'S PAST!

https://www.subscribepage.com/fireheart

About the author:

Connor Whiteley is the author of over 60 books in the sci-fi fantasy, nonfiction psychology and books for writer's genre and he is a Human Branding Speaker and Consultant.

He is a passionate warhammer 40,000 reader, psychology student and author.

Who narrates his own audiobooks and he hosts The Psychology World Podcast.

All whilst studying Psychology at the University of Kent, England.

Also, he was a former Explorer Scout where he gave a speech to the Maltese President in August 2018 and he attended Prince Charles' 70th Birthday Party at Buckingham Palace in May 2018.

Plus, he is a self-confessed coffee lover!

Other books by Connor Whiteley:

Bettie English Private Eye Series
A Very Private Woman
The Russian Case
A Very Urgent Matter
A Case Most Personal
Trains, Scots and Private Eyes
The Federation Protects

Lord of War Origin Trilogy:
Not Scared Of The Dark
Madness
Burn Them All

The Fireheart Fantasy Series
Heart of Fire
Heart of Lies
Heart of Prophecy
Heart of Bones
Heart of Fate

City of Assassins (Urban Fantasy)
City of Death
City of Marytrs
City of Pleasure
City of Power

Agents of The Emperor
Return of The Ancient Ones
Vigilance

Angels of Fire
Kingmaker
The Eight
The Lost Generation
Hunt
Emperor's Council
Speaker of Treachery
Birth Of The Empire
Terraforma

Lord Of War Trilogy (Agents of The Emperor)
Not Scared Of The Dark
Madness
Burn It All Down

The Garro Series- Fantasy/Sci-fi
GARRO: GALAXY'S END
GARRO: RISE OF THE ORDER
GARRO: END TIMES
GARRO: SHORT STORIES
GARRO: COLLECTION
GARRO: HERESY
GARRO: FAITHLESS
GARRO: DESTROYER OF WORLDS
GARRO: COLLECTIONS BOOK 4-6
GARRO: MISTRESS OF BLOOD
GARRO: BEACON OF HOPE
GARRO: END OF DAYS

<u>Winter Series- Fantasy Trilogy Books</u>
WINTER'S COMING
WINTER'S HUNT
WINTER'S REVENGE
WINTER'S DISSENSION

<u>Miscellaneous:</u>
RETURN
FREEDOM
SALVATION
Reflection of Mount Flame
The Masked One
The Great Deer

<u>Gay Romance Novellas</u>
Breaking, Nursing, Repairing A Broken Heart
Jacob And Daniel
Fallen For A Lie
Spying And Weddings

OTHER SHORT STORIES BY CONNOR WHITELEY

<u>Mystery Short Story Collections</u>

Criminally Good Stories Volume 1: 20 Detective Mystery Short Stories

Criminally Good Stories Volume 2: 20 Private Investigator Short Stories

Criminally Good Stories Volume 3: 20 Crime Fiction Short Stories

Criminally Good Stories Volume 4: 20 Science Fiction and Fantasy Mystery Short Stories

Criminally Good Stories Volume 5: 20 Romantic Suspense Short Stories

<u>Mystery Short Stories:</u>

Protecting The Woman She Hated

Finding A Royal Friend

Our Woman In Paris

Corrupt Driving

A Prime Assassination

Jubilee Thief

Jubilee, Terror, Celebrations

Negative Jubilation

Ghostly Jubilation

Killing For Womenkind

A Snowy Death

Miracle Of Death

A Spy In Rome

The 12:30 To St Pancreas

A Country In Trouble

A Smokey Way To Go
A Spicy Way To GO
A Marketing Way To Go
A Missing Way To Go
A Showering Way To Go
Poison In The Candy Cane
Christmas Innocence
You Better Watch Out
Christmas Theft
Trouble In Christmas
Smell of The Lake
Problem In A Car
Theft, Past and Team
Embezzler In The Room
A Strange Way To Go
A Horrible Way To Go
Ann Awful Way To Go
An Old Way To Go
A Fishy Way To Go
A Pointy Way To Go
A High Way To Go
A Fiery Way To Go
A Glassy Way To Go
A Chocolatey Way To Go
Kendra Detective Mystery Collection Volume 1
Kendra Detective Mystery Collection Volume 2
Stealing A Chance At Freedom
Glassblowing and Death
Theft of Independence
Cookie Thief

Marble Thief
Book Thief
Art Thief
Mated At The Morgue
The Big Five Whoopee Moments
Stealing An Election
Mystery Short Story Collection Volume 1
Mystery Short Story Collection Volume 2
Criminal Performance
Candy Detectives
Key To Birth In The Past

Science Fiction Short Stories:
Temptation
Superhuman Autospy
Blood In The Redwater
All Is Dust
Vigil
Emperor Forgive Us
Their Brave New World
Gummy Bear Detective
The Candy Detective
What Candies Fear
The Blurred Image
Shattered Legions
The First Rememberer
Life of A Rememberer
System of Wonder
Lifesaver
Remarkable Way She Died

The Interrogation of Annabella Stormic
Blade of The Emperor
Arbiter's Truth
Computation of Battle
Old One's Wrath
Puppets and Masters
Ship of Plague
Interrogation
Edge of Failure
One Way Choice
Acceptable Losses
Balance of Power
Good Idea At The Time
Escape Plan
Escape In The Hesitation
Inspiration In Need
Singing Warriors
Knowledge is Power
Killer of Polluters
Climate of Death
The Family Mailing Affair
Defining Criminality
The Martian Affair
A Cheating Affair
The Little Café Affair
Mountain of Death
Prisoner's Fight
Claws of Death
Bitter Air
Honey Hunt

Blade On A Train

<u>Fantasy Short Stories:</u>

City of Snow

City of Light

City of Vengeance

Dragons, Goats and Kingdom

Smog The Pathetic Dragon

Don't Go In The Shed

The Tomato Saver

The Remarkable Way She Died

The Bloodied Rose

Asmodia's Wrath

Heart of A Killer

Emissary of Blood

Dragon Coins

Dragon Tea

Dragon Rider

Sacrifice of the Soul

Heart of The Flesheater

Heart of The Regent

Heart of The Standing

Feline of The Lost

Heart of The Story

City of Fire

Awaiting Death

All books in 'An Introductory Series':
Careers In Psychology
Psychology of Suicide
Dementia Psychology
Forensic Psychology of Terrorism And Hostage-Taking
Forensic Psychology of False Allegations
Year In Psychology
BIOLOGICAL PSYCHOLOGY 3RD EDITION
COGNITIVE PSYCHOLOGY THIRD EDITION
SOCIAL PSYCHOLOGY- 3RD EDITION
ABNORMAL PSYCHOLOGY 3RD EDITION
PSYCHOLOGY OF RELATIONSHIPS- 3RD EDITION
DEVELOPMENTAL PSYCHOLOGY 3RD EDITION
HEALTH PSYCHOLOGY
RESEARCH IN PSYCHOLOGY
A GUIDE TO MENTAL HEALTH AND TREATMENT AROUND THE WORLD- A GLOBAL LOOK AT DEPRESSION
FORENSIC PSYCHOLOGY
THE FORENSIC PSYCHOLOGY OF THEFT, BURGLARY AND OTHER CRIMES AGAINST PROPERTY
CRIMINAL PROFILING: A FORENSIC PSYCHOLOGY GUIDE TO FBI PROFILING AND GEOGRAPHICAL AND STATISTICAL PROFILING.
CLINICAL PSYCHOLOGY

CONNOR WHITELEY

FORMULATION IN PSYCHOTHERAPY
PERSONALITY PSYCHOLOGY AND INDIVIDUAL DIFFERENCES
CLINICAL PSYCHOLOGY REFLECTIONS VOLUME 1
CLINICAL PSYCHOLOGY REFLECTIONS VOLUME 2
Clinical Psychology Reflections Volume 3
CULT PSYCHOLOGY
Police Psychology

A Psychology Student's Guide To University
How Does University Work?
A Student's Guide To University And Learning
University Mental Health and Mindset